HOTEL TRANSYLVANIA

PAPERCUTZ™

MORE GREAT GRAPHIC NOVEL SERIES AVAILABLE FROM PAPERCUTZ

THE SMURFS #21

THE GARFIELD SHOW #6

BARBIE #1

BARBIE PUPPY PARTY

TROLLS #1

GERONIMO STILTON #17

THEA STILTON #6

NANCY DREW DIARIES #7

THE LUNCH WITCH #1

SCARLETT

ANNE OF GREEN BAGELS #1

DRACULA MARRIES FRANKENSTEIN!

THE RED SHOES

THE LITTLE MERMAID

FUZZY BASEBALL

HOTEL TRANSYLVANIA #1

THE LOUD HOUSE #1

MANOSAURS #1

THE ONLY LIVING BOY #5

HOTEL TRANSYLVANIA
KAKIELAND KATASTROPHE

STEFAN PETRUCHA—WRITER

ALLEN GLADFELTER—ARTIST

PAPERCUTZ

NEW YORK

#1 Kakieland Katastrophe
Stefan Petrucha—Writer
Allen Gladfelter—Artist
Laurie E. Smith—Colorist [pages 1-30]
Matt Herms—Colorist [pages 31-50]
Wilson Ramos Jr.—Letterer
Production—Dawn Guzzo
Assistant Managing Editor—Jeff Whitman
Jim Salicrup
Editor-in-Chief

Special Thanks to James Silvani, Keith Baxter, Melissa Sturm,
Virginia King and everyone at Sony Pictures Animation

ISBN: 978-1-62991-808-2 paperback edition
ISBN: 978-1-62991-809-9 hardcover edition

Sony Pictures Animation

Papercutz books may be purchased for business or promotional
use. For information on bulk purchases please contact Macmillan
Corporate and Premium Sales Department at
(800) 221-795 x5442.

Printed in USA
September 2017

Distributed by Macmillan
First Printing

HOTEL TRANSYLVANIA

DRAC

Legendary monster, hotelier
extraordinaire and loving father,
Drac is finally enjoying the perks
of a monster AND human filled
Hotel Transylvania. Running
your own business can be a
pain in the neck but running a
family business along with being
the most legendary monster in
history is biting off a little more
than he can chew! But luckily
he's got the trusty Drac Pack by
his side and his loyal and ever-
loving daughter, Mavis.

MAVIS

Juggling work at Hotel Transylvania and being an awesome mother, wife and daughter, Mavis does it all! She's curious, optimistic and deeply loyal to her monster and human family. While she relishes being her own vampire, she will always be daddy's little bat.

HOTEL TRANSYLVANIA

FRANK

Frank is a guy who will always leave you in stitches! He's one of Drac's best friends and is always there to lend a hand, or an arm or a leg.

HOTEL TRANSYLVANIA

MURRAY

Murray is literally the firmly wrapped fixture of the Drac Pack...because he's a mummy! He is the life of the party and is always there in a pinch to bandage any problem Drac may have.

HOTEL TRANSYLVANIA

DENNIS

All vampires have until their fifth
birthday to sprout their fangs...
and wouldn't you know it...
Mavis and Johnny's son did!
Dennis is a curly-haired, curious
kid, who just wants to sneak off
and have adventures with his
best wolf pup friend, Winnie.

HOTEL TRANSYLVANIA

JOHNNY

Marrying into any family can be scary but marrying into THIS family is thrilling! Not only was he the first human ever to set foot into Hotel Transylvania but he married Mavis and they had a beautiful son together named Dennis. Johnny is even getting his overly skeptical father-in-law to soften up on him. It's a crazy life Johnny has stumbled into but he takes it all in stride...backpack and all.

HOTEL TRANSYLVANIA

WAYNE

Wayne, the werewolf, would love to be howling at the moon but he has no time! He's got a gazillion wolf pups along with his wife Wanda of which to take care. In his little free time, Wayne enjoys teaching tennis and playing fetch at the same time as well as rocking the bass!

HOTEL TRANSYLVANIA

WINNIE

She's one of Wayne and Wanda's numerous pups. She's wild, rambunctious and always game for a mischievous adventure. She also has a not-so-secret crush on Dennis.

HOTEL TRANSYLVANIA

BLOBBY

This blob monster is always wiggling and
jiggling for a good time! Semi-transparent
and unassuming, Blobby is the one friend
that everyone counts on in the group.
He's even his own lost and found—
you never know what you'll
find in his goo!

THE END

WATCH OUT FOR PAPERCUTZ™

Welcome to HOTEL TRANSYLVANIA, or more accurately, welcome to the premiere HOTEL TRANSYLVANIA graphic novel, by Stefan Petrucha, writer, and Allen Gladfelter, artist, from Papercutz—those monstrously-talented madmen and women dedicated to publishing graphic novels for all ages. I'm Jim Salicrup, Editor-in-Chief and part-time room service employee at the HOTEL TRANSYLVANIA. I'm here to share a personal behind-the-scenes story, recommend a few monstrous Papercutz graphic novels, and offer up some HOTEL TRANSYLVANIA news, in that order…

Longtime Papercutz fans may know that writer Stefan Petrucha and I were childhood friends. I have many great memories of us making comics together when we were kids, but we were also fans of monsters. We loved all sorts of monster stories, monster movies, monster TV shows, and, of course, monster comicbooks. Stefan, I think, loved monsters even more than I did. While after school I would often watch *The Mike Douglas Show*, a talk show that would feature guests such as Moe Howard of the Three Stooges and John Lennon of the Beatles, Stefan was a faithful fan of *Dark Shadows*, a soap opera that featured vampires and werewolves. Together, we've seen many a Frankenstein movie over the years, and Stefan even wrote the novel *"The Shadow of Frankenstein,"* an official sequel to the classic Frankenstein film starring Boris Karloff, so when it came time to choose the perfect comics writer for the HOTEL TRANSYLVANIA, I didn't have to think twice—Stefan is my go-to Monster-Writer! To learn more about Stefan, check out his website at www.petrucha.com.

At Papercutz, we've enjoyed publishing all sorts of graphic novels featuring monsters. We published a series of CLASSICS ILLUSTRATED graphic novels—one series featured 48-page adaptations, and the other featured far-longer comics adaptations of these classic novels: In CLASSICS ILLUSTRATED #2, we featured H.G. Wells's "The Invisible Man," adapted by Rick Geary; in #4, Edgar Allan Poe's "The Raven and Other Poems," illustrated by Gahan Wilson; in #7, Robert Louis Stevenson's "Dr. Jekyll & Mr. Hyde," adapted by John K. Snyder III; and in #12, H.G. Wells's "The Island of Dr. Moreau," adapted by Steven Grant and Eric Vincent. In CLASSICS ILLUSTRATED DELUXE #3, Mary Shelley's "Frankenstein," adapted by Marion Mousse; and in #10, Edgar Allan Poe's "The Murders in the Rue Morgue and Other Tales," adapted by Morvan & Druet, and Corbeyran & Marcel. We also published four funny MONSTER graphic novels by brilliant cartoonist Lewis Trondheim, in which a special powder is able to bring any drawing, especially those of monsters, to life. Many of these great graphic novels may now be out-of-print, but worth finding at your local library. Easier to find are the more recent Papercutz graphic novels such as the two volumes of THE LUNCH WITCH by Deb Lucke, about an out-of-work witch who decides to make ends meet by becoming a school lunch lady. And there's DRACULA MARRIES FRANKENSTEIN, the latest *Anne of Green Bagels* graphic novel by Susan Schade and John Buller, about Anne and her friend Otto spending their summer making a funny monster movie.

Which brings us back to the HOTEL TRANSYLVANIA movies… These movies have been so popular that HOTEL TRANSYLVANIA 3 is being released in July 2018. But the HOTEL TRANSYLVANIA story doesn't end there (or here)! Now airing on the Disney Channel is an all-new animated TV series inspired by the HOTEL TRANSYLVANIA movies, and Papercutz is proud to announce that we'll be creating all-new graphic novels, by Stefan Petrucha and Allen Gladfelter, inspired by the TV series! So, if you love Drac, Mavis, Frank, Murray, Wayne, and all the rest, as much as we do, this is the greatest news of all! The TV series is actually expanding the HOTEL TRANSYLVANIA universe in a way we're sure you're going to enjoy, and we can't wait for you to experience it! So until the next HOTEL TRANSYLVANIA graphic novel (coming soon!), this is your Papercutz Editor-in-Chief saying "Bleh, bleh, bleh!"

Thanks,

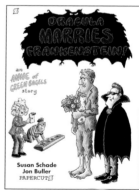

STAY IN TOUCH!

EMAIL: salicrup@papercutz.com
WEB: papercutz.com
INSTAGRAM: @papercutzgn
TWITTER: @papercutzgn
FACEBOOK: PAPERCUTZGRAPHICNOVELS
FAN MAIL: Papercutz, 160 Broadway, Suite 700, East Wing, New York, NY 10038